ON THE GHOST TRAIL

CHRIS POWLING
ILLUSTRATED BY LORETTA SCHAUER

BLOOMSBURY EDUCATION
LONDON   OXFORD   NEW YORK   NEW DELHI   SYDNEY

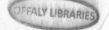

BLOOMSBURY EDUCATION
Bloomsbury Publishing Plc
50 Bedford Square, London, WC1B 3DP, UK
29 Earlsfort Terrace, Dublin 2, Ireland

BLOOMSBURY, BLOOMSBURY EDUCATION and the Diana logo
are trademarks of Bloomsbury Publishing Plc

First published in Great Britain in 2006 by A&C Black, an imprint
of Bloomsbury Publishing Plc

This edition published in 2022 by Bloomsbury Publishing Plc

Text copyright © Chris Powling, 2006
Illustrations copyright © Loretta Schauer, 2020

Packaged for Bloomsbury by Plum5 Limited

Chris Powling and Loretta Schauer have asserted their rights under the Copyright,
Designs and Patents Act, 1988, to be identified as Author and Illustrator of this work

A catalogue record for this book is available from the British Library

ISBN: PB: 978-1-4729-6735-0; ePDF: 978-1-4729-6734-3;
ePub: 978-1-4729-6732-9

2 4 6 8 10 9 7 5 3

Printed and bound by CPI Group (UK) Ltd, Croydon, CR20 4YY

MIX
Paper from
responsible sources
FSC® C013604

To find out more about our authors and books visit www.bloomsbury.com and sign up for our newsletters

CONTENTS

Chapter One   5

Chapter Two   13

Chapter Three   19

Chapter Four   32

Chapter Five   41

For Polly...
as good as a little sister gets

CHAPTER ONE

Grandpa's house is a bit like
Grandpa. It's so old and creaky,
you see. Also, it's rather untidy
in a Grandpa-like kind of way.

"My house reminds me of *me*,"
he always says.

It reminds us of Grandpa, too.
No wonder we love to stay there.
At least, we did till our visit last
spring. That's when my big brother
Adam started to wind us up.

"Look!" he exclaimed one tea time. "See those cobwebs, Ben?"

"Cobwebs?" I said.

"In the fireplace." Adam pointed. "Where the bricks have gone all smoky. How do you think they got there?"

"Spiders, I suppose," I said.

"No," said Adam. "Not spiders…"

"Not spiders?" said Susie, our little sister. "They look like spider webs to me."

Adam shook his head. "They may *look* like spider webs, Susie. But really it's a ghost trail."

"A ghost trail?" I said.

"Exactly. A ghost was slipping up the chimney, I expect. Probably it brushed against the brickwork. That cobwebby-looking stuff is a little bit of ghost that got left behind."

Susie and I stared at the fireplace. Was it really a ghost trail hanging there? Or were they just ordinary, everyday cobwebs that Grandpa hadn't spotted?

Luckily, Grandpa came in just then with our tea. He noticed how quiet we were at once.

"Anything wrong, kids?" he asked.

"It's Adam," said Susie. "He was telling us—"

"About those cobwebs," Adam cut in.

Grandpa squinted at the fireplace. "Oh dear," he said. "My eyes aren't what they used to be, I'm afraid. This place is getting grubby. I hope it won't put you off your food."

"No chance," said Adam.

After this, we got busy with the buns. Grandpa joined in, too.

Susie took a picture of us all with the digital camera she'd got for her birthday. Everything was back to normal in Grandpa's creaky old house.

Almost normal, anyway.

There was still the ghost trail in the fireplace, I mean.

CHAPTER TWO

At bedtime, Adam teased us again.

His voice floated down from the top bunk. It was just loud enough for us to hear every word – me in the bunk below him, Susie in her bed over by the window.

"Ben," whispered Adam. "There it is again. Can you hear it?"

"Hear what?" I asked.

"*That,*" said Adam.

Which noise did he mean,
though? At night you can hear lots
of noises in a house as old and
creaky as Grandpa's.

We could
hear the wind
moaning in the
chimney. We
could hear the
rumble of the
washing machine
downstairs. We

could hear the yip of a fox at the
bottom of the garden.

But Adam
wasn't talking
about these.

TAP–TAP–TAP

"OK," I said. "What is it?"

"A twig," said Susie. "It's a twig, that's all. Just a twig tapping against the windowpane."

"Yes, it *could* be a twig," said Adam. "It *sounds* like a twig, I agree. Unless it's a ghost's heartbeat, of course."

"A ghost's heartbeat?" I gasped.

"How can it be a ghost's heartbeat?" said Susie. "A ghost is already dead. It hasn't got a heartbeat."

"Exactly," said Adam. "That's what makes it so scary. Probably it's the same ghost that left the trail in the fireplace. Still, let's pretend it's just a twig. Goodnight, Ben! Goodnight, Susie!"

TAP–TAP–TAP

How could we possibly sleep after that?

CHAPTER THREE

Next day it was raining hard.
We spent the morning curled up
with books and comics.

Grandpa's creaky, old house had never felt more cosy. I almost forgot about the ghost trail. I almost forgot about the ghost's heartbeat as well.

After lunch, the sun came out.

"Leave the
washing-up
to me, kids,"
Grandpa said.
"This sunshine
may not last.
Go outside for
a good, brisk
walk while you can!"

"Your special walk, Grandpa?"
asked Susie.

"If you like," Grandpa said.
"Can you remember the way?"

We all laughed at that.
Grandpa had shown us his special
walk hundreds of times.

First, we would cross the garden
as far as the hole in his hedge.
Then came the long, winding path
round the church next door.

After this, we took a short cut
back through the graveyard till
we arrived at Grandpa's front
door again.

"You'll be safe enough in daylight," Grandpa told us. "There's no need to hurry. Stop for a look and a listen every now and then."

"Exactly!" Adam grinned. "We'll look and listen every step of the way, Grandpa!"

He didn't have to say what for. Not after all his teasing yesterday. We'd be looking for ghost trails, that's what. And we'd be listening for ghostly heartbeats as well.

Thanks, Adam.

At first, everything was fresh and sparkling on Grandpa's special walk. I'd never seen Susie take so many pictures.

Of course, I guessed what she was up to. The camera was helping her shut out the ghost trail.

This cobweb dripping with raindrops, for instance. Was it a ghost dressed up for a party? Or that *tap–tap–tap* of the blossom against the church porch. Were a couple of ghosts getting married?

Wherever I looked and listened, springtime seemed full of ghosts.

And it was all my big brother's
fault.

Can you blame us for hanging
back? At least it meant Susie and
I could talk.

"What's wrong with Adam?"
I asked her. "Why this spooky
stuff all of a sudden?"

"What spooky stuff?" said Susie.

"You know – the cobwebs and tapping and suchlike. I suppose you think we should take no notice!"

"Exactly," said Susie.

I was amazed. Honestly, she sounded just like our big brother! Sometimes I can hardly believe she's the baby of the family.

"OK," I said. "But suppose taking no notice doesn't work. What do we do then?"

"We scare him back," said my little sister.

Scare him back?

We *were* talking about Adam, weren't we? He's two years older than I am – and four years older than Susie. How can you possibly scare your big brother?

Already, when we caught up with him, I saw that teasing glint in his eye.

"Midnight," he grinned.

"Midnight?" I said.

"Midnight tonight, yes. Here in the graveyard. When the church clock is striking twelve. That's the best time to hunt down this ghost of ours. Are you two up for it?"

"Count me out," said Susie. "Who wants to hang around in a graveyard after dark? There's no fun in that. I'd rather be tucked up in bed, thank you."

"How about you, Ben?"

"Me?"

"Yes, you. Are you frightened as well?"

Adam was looking at me now in his most big-brotherly way. He was expecting me to agree with Susie, I think. And that's what I should have done, of course.

I still don't know why I didn't.

CHAPTER FOUR

It was nearly midnight. Adam and I slipped quietly out of bed. We dressed without a word. Then we crossed the bedroom on tiptoe.

Susie didn't say goodbye.
I guessed she was already fast
asleep.

Tonight there was no wind at
all. No rumble from the washing
machine, either. The old staircase
hardly creaked as we crept
downstairs. Out in the garden,
we checked for foxes.

"Can't see a single one," said my
big brother. "They must be having a
night off."

"Lucky foxes," I gulped.

"You scared, Ben?"

"Aren't you?"

"Nah…"

My big brother sounded
scared, though. This should have
made me feel better, I suppose.
Instead, I was more nervous than
ever as we stumbled across the
garden. It took us ages to find the
gap in the hedge.

"Keep the torch still, Adam,"
I hissed. "You're making it flicker all
over the place."

"You hold it then!"

"No, not me."

I didn't fancy seeing the ghost first. Maybe Adam didn't, either. Even the shadows seemed to have a shadow now... or something pretending to be a shadow.

Something as black as a vampire, perhaps. Or as hairy as a werewolf.

"Stay close to me, Ben," said my brother. "We mustn't split up, OK?"

"You bet," I said.

The torch swung madly this way and that as we followed the path round the church. Its beam seemed to get more and more feeble with every step we took. Then, in the middle of the graveyard, it went out altogether.

Adam let out a groan. "The battery's gone!" he said. "I can't see a thing!"

"You're not the only one!" I croaked.

We hadn't lost our ears, though. Especially when the church clock started to strike.

DONG! DONG! DONG!

Midnight was all around us now.
So were the shadows. It was as if they
were ganging up on us – an ambush
of shadows. Had the darkness been
lying in wait to duff us up?

As the last of the chimes faded, we both sighed with relief. But the worst wasn't over yet. Not by a long shot. Already we could hear another sound.

TAP–TAP–TAP

I could almost feel how close it was – like the prod of a bony finger. Like the jab of a bony elbow. Like the beat of a bony heart in a tangle of cobwebs.

The sound was forcing me to turn round. Adam was turning round, too.

TAP–TAP–TAP

Luckily, the dazzle was too
small to blind us. It was more like a
firework exploding in your face. Or a
light sabre slashing at your nose.

It was the shock of it that made
us run.

Adam only just beat me out of the graveyard. I may even have reached Grandpa's front door ahead of him. Don't ask me how we scrambled inside without waking the whole house. We spent the rest of the night on the sofa downstairs. Neither of us dared go up to bed. Just one creak from that old staircase would have freaked us out.

CHAPTER FIVE

That's where Grandpa found us
next morning. He
poked his head
round the door
and winked.
"Sleeping on
the sofa, eh?
Anything to
do with last
night's little
adventure?"

"Adventure?" I said.

"How do you know about that?" Adam asked.

Grandpa tapped his nose. "I don't miss very much, you know – apart from the odd cobweb here and there. Want to tell me what was going on out there in the dark?"

So we did.

And not just about the ambush, either. Somehow, we talked about the ghost trail as well. Also about teasing and being teased.

Grandpa told us that the problem with teasing was knowing when to stop.

"Hear what I'm saying, Adam?" he said.

"Yes," said Adam, going red.

"Good," said Grandpa. "Mind you, there's been a lot of teasing going on round here. Have you any idea where this came from?"

He held out a photo.

It had been taken with a digital camera, probably. Then printed out from Grandpa's computer.

We could see every single detail, I promise you – the church, the gravestones, our mouths gaping wide in horror. Midnight was as clear as day in the picture. It always is when you use a flash.

A *flash*?

So that's what had shocked us.

"Did you take this, Grandpa?" Adam said. "Were you following us all the time?"

"Me?" said Grandpa. "At my time of life? I'm much too old and creaky to chase a couple of kids round a graveyard – especially after dark. I gave up that sort of caper years ago. Maybe it was the ghost who caught you on camera!"

"It must have been," said Adam, quickly.

"Yeah!" I agreed.

After all, who else could it be?

Surely not a kid who was two years younger than me and four years younger than my brother... a kid brave enough to follow us into a graveyard at the dead of night.

It's easier to believe in a ghost than in a little sister like that.

Isn't it?